My Puppy Patch

by Theo Heras

Illustrations by Alice Carter

pajamapress

Today, Patch and I will walk to the corner. This will be her first time outside the fence.

But first, we have to practice our commands.

"Patch, sit," I
say. And she sits.

"Patch, down," I say.
And she lies down.

"Patch, stay," I say.
And she doesn't move.

But before I can
give her a treat...

...Patch discovers dandelions!

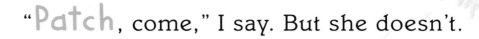

"Patch, come," I say. But she doesn't.

"Patch...*come*," I say more firmly.

Patch looks at me with big, sad eyes.

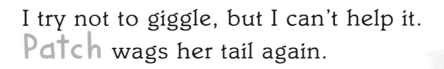

I try not to giggle, but I can't help it. Patch wags her tail again.

"All right," I say. "We can practice that one later. Patch, stay."

And she stays. I attach Patch's leash to her collar and open the gate.

Patch is so excited, she...

...rolls over...

...wags...

...yips...

...and leaps for joy.

At last, we set off down the street.

Patch loves to explore…

…butterflies…

…bugs…

...and puddles!

I know she isn't supposed to tug on her leash,
so I stop walking and say, "Patch, come."

And she does!

I see Benny at the end of the street.
He has a new puppy too.

"Hey, Benny," I call. "Patch has
had all her shots now. What about
your puppy?"

Benny laughs. "I didn't like seeing
those needles, but Smallfry
wasn't afraid at all."

We reach the end of the street. The two puppies sniff each other.

"**Smallfry**?" I say with a grin.

"Wait till he grows up," says Benny.

The two puppies leap…

…and roll…

…and tussle.

Soon their leashes are tangled.

"Time to go," I say. "Patch, sit." And she does!

"Wow!" Benny says. "Patch is pretty smart."

After we untangle their leashes, I give Patch a treat and we walk back proudly.

But when **Patch** finds a REALLY muddy puddle,
she jumps right in...

...and splashes...

...and rolls...

...and shakes

mud all over me!

At home, I wipe her feet, rub her down, and tickle her tummy. But now I need a towel too!

Patch will want a drink of water. And her bed is nearby when she is ready for a nap.

Soon it will be time for her supper.

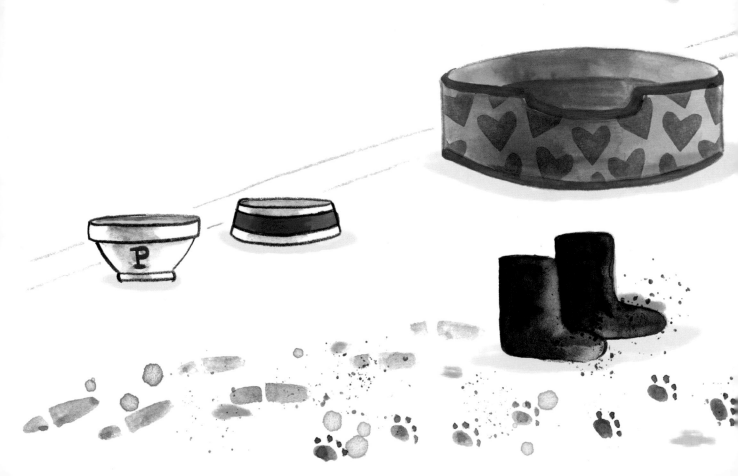

"Patch, I love you," I whisper.
"You are the best puppy ever."

First published in Canada and the United States in 2019

Text copyright © 2019 Theo Heras
Illustration copyright © 2019 Alice Carter
This edition copyright © 2019 Pajama Press Inc.
This is a first edition.

www.pajamapress.ca   info@pajamapress.ca

 Canada Council Conseil des arts
for the Arts du Canada

 ONTARIO ARTS COUNCIL
CONSEIL DES ARTS DE L'ONTARIO
an Ontario government agency
un organisme du gouvernement de l'Ontario

 Canadä

The publisher gratefully acknowledges the support of the Canada Council for the Arts and the Ontario Arts Council for its publishing program. We acknowledge the financial support of the Government of Canada through the Canada Book Fund (CBF) for our publishing activities.

Library and Archives Canada Cataloguing in Publication

Heras, Theo, 1948-, author
     My puppy patch / by Theo Heras ; illustrations by Alice Carter. -- First edition.
ISBN 978-1-77278-080-2 (hardcover)
     1. Puppies--Training--Juvenile literature. 2. Human-animal relationships--
Juvenile literature. I. Carter, Alice, illustrator II. Title.
SF431.H47 2019   j636.7'0887   C2018-905914-1

Publisher Cataloging-in-Publication Data (U.S.)

Names: Heras, Theo, 1948-, author. | Carter, Alice, 1977-, illustrator.
Title: My Puppy Patch / by Theo Heras ; illustrations by Alice Carter.
Description: Toronto, Ontario Canada : Pajama Press, 2019. | Summary: "A young girl takes her new puppy out for its first walk beyond the garden gate, teaching the dog such commands as "sit," "stay," and "down" in this simple story for young readers that introduces basics of pet ownership and training"— Provided by publisher.
Identifiers: ISBN 978-1-77278-080-2 (hardcover)
Subjects: LCSH: Puppies -- Training -- Juvenile fiction. | Responsibility – Juvenile fiction. | Pets – Juvenile fiction. | BISAC: JUVENILE FICTION / Animals / Dogs. | JUVENILE FICTION / Social Themes / Friendship. | JUVENILE FICTION / Social Themes / New Experience.
Classification: LCC PZ7.H473My |DDC [E] – dc23

Original art created with colored pencil, watercolor, and digital media
Cover and book design—Rebecca Bender

Manufactured by Qualibre Inc./Printplus
Printed in China

Pajama Press Inc.
181 Carlaw Ave. Suite 251 Toronto, Ontario Canada, M4M 2S1

Distributed in Canada by UTP Distribution
5201 Dufferin Street Toronto, Ontario Canada, M3H 5T8

Distributed in the U.S. by Ingram Publisher Services
1 Ingram Blvd. La Vergne, TN 37086, USA

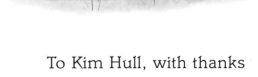

To Kim Hull, with thanks
—T.H.

For ZP and PM,
and all the dogs we've loved
—A.C.